Disney's POCAHONTAS

HELLO, FUNNY FACE

By Margo Lundell

Illustrated by Jose Cardona and Josie Yee

A GOLDEN BOOK • NEW YORK
Western Publishing Company, Inc., Racine, Wisconsin 53404

Before European settlers came to Virginia, an Indian girl named Pocahontas was growing up there with her tribe. One year her mother grew sick and died. Months passed, but Pocahontas was still sad.

On a day late in summer her father, Chief Powhatan, urged her to go with her friends and practice for the harvest races.

Pocahontas sighed. "Father, I don't think I want to be a runner this year," she answered.

It was clear that the girl needed more time before she could be herself again.

When Powhatan was gone, Flit the hummingbird came
to visit. He saw Pocahontas's beadwork lying next to her,
untouched. Flit picked up a bead and tossed it to her
playfully. Then he picked up another and another.

"All right, Flit! I will do my work," said Pocahontas
with a smile. "You're right. It's good to be busy."

Soon Pocahontas's friend Nakoma stopped by. She had
been in the fields, picking wildflowers.

She put one in Pocahontas's hair. "Flowers are magic,"
said Nakoma. "They make everyone feel better."

"Thank you, my good friend," said Pocahontas.

Then Pocahontas went to visit Grandmother Willow.
The old woman was an ancient tree spirit, full of wisdom
and love for Pocahontas.

"Everyone is worrying about me, Grandmother," said Pocahontas. "They don't want me to be sad anymore."

"Everything is happening the way it should," said Grandmother Willow. "Your sadness will go away when your heart can once again be touched."

The next day Nakoma talked Pocahontas into going on a canoe trip. They planned to go upriver to a place where wild cherries grew.

"The ripe cherries are just waiting for us," said Nakoma. "You'll see."

After the two had paddled for a while, the river grew
narrow and the water ran faster. Suddenly Pocahontas
heard a shrill crying sound above the rushing water.
  "Do you hear something?" asked Pocahontas.
Nakoma shook her head.

The sound was coming from a young raccoon in trouble.
He was clinging to a branch racing downstream.

"I see an animal caught in the current!" Pocahontas called
to Nakoma. "Steer to the right while I try to rescue him."

By the time Pocahontas pulled the raccoon out of the water,
he was exhausted. She put him in a basket and went back to
her paddling.

Soon they reached the place where the cherry trees grew and went ashore. Before Pocahontas began picking cherries, she carried the raccoon to a sunny spot.

"Rest now," she told the little animal. "I'll be back."

By the end of the day, Pocahontas had decided to take the raccoon home with her. She named him Meeko.

On the day after his rescue, Meeko was weak and tired.
Pocahontas tried to feed him, but the raccoon wouldn't eat.
"Your stomach doesn't want food," said Pocahontas, patting
Meeko gently. "But your eyes follow me wherever I go."

That night Meeko became very ill. He seemed to have
a fever. Pocahontas knew he must drink water to live.
Nakoma came to the longhouse to help Pocahontas.
"Drink, Meeko, drink," urged Pocahontas.

By morning Meeko was feeling better. When Flit brought berries from a nearby bush, Meeko gobbled them down.

"In a few days he will go back to the forest," Pocahontas told Nakoma. "I will miss him."

Soon Meeko grew stronger, but he did not go back to the forest. He stayed with Pocahontas.

"He follows me everywhere," the girl told her father.

"Yes—like a second shadow!" Powhatan said, laughing.

After that, Meeko rarely left Pocahontas's side. The little
raccoon was a real clown. And Flit could be counted on to
scold Meeko when he thought the silly raccoon was going
too far with his antics.

Day after day the two creatures made Pocahontas laugh.

Finally Pocahontas took Meeko to meet Grandmother
Willow. While they were there, Meeko began to play.
Soon Pocahontas was smiling at the little raccoon.
"You are happier now," said Grandmother Willow.
"You have let this little funny face touch your heart."

It was almost harvesttime, a season for celebrating.
Pocahontas decided to run in the races, after all. To prepare,
she ran through the forest each day like a young deer.

"Hurry up, Meeko!" she called. "We don't want to be left
behind."

On the day of the games everyone was excited. Later there would be a feast and dancing. The winners of the races would sit in special places by the tribal fire.

With Meeko at her side, Pocahontas waited to begin the first race. Everyone knew she ran like the wind. It would be hard to catch her.

"Ready," said the chief. "Go!"

The sprint was over. "The winner is Pocahontas!" said Powhatan. "And Meeko the raccoon."

As everyone cheered, Meeko sat proudly on Pocahontas's shoulder. Pocahontas thanked the spirits for sending him into her life.